THE
HUNTER

Anne Schraff

PAGETURNERS

ADVENTURE

A Horse Called Courage

Planet Doom

The Terrible Orchid Sky

Up Rattler Mountain

Who Has Seen the Beast?

MYSTERY

The Hunter

Once Upon a Crime

Whatever Happened
to Megan Marie?

When Sleeping Dogs Awaken

Where's Dudley?

Development and Production: Laurel Associates, Inc.
Cover Illustrator: Black Eagle Productions

SADDLEBACK
PUBLISHING • INC.

Three Watson
Irvine, CA 92618-2767

E-Mail: info@sdlback.com
Website: www.sdlback.com

ISBN 1-56254-181-1

Printed in the United States of America
05 04 03 02 01 00   9 8 7 6 5 4 3 2 1

CONTENTS

Chapter 1

Greg Naylor was pitching balls to his buddy, Tommy Wilkins, on the diamond at Evergreen High School. Twilight was quickly turning into darkness, but Greg tried to practice his pitching every chance he got.

Greg had graduated from Evergreen High School four years ago. Now he worked as an electrician for a local contractor, and he was making good money. It was a good enough job, but Greg had never completely given up on his dream of playing baseball for a living. He kept having fantasies about open tryouts where he'd show up and be so good they'd offer him a contract.

"You're nuts, man," Tommy would laugh when Greg talked about his dream. "The baseball players today, they get picked *young,* right out of high school or college. There are so many talented kids that some latecomer like you ain't got much of a chance!"

Greg laughed. "You don't know what you're talking about. When I'm making megabucks in the majors you're gonna need a gallon of mayo to help you eat your words!" Greg wasn't bitter about missing out on the baseball draft. An ankle injury had sidelined him during his senior year—and that was that. He had led the Evergreen Raiders to two championships before the injury.

Greg was only 22 now. He thought he still had a fair chance to join a farm club. Then, if he proved he had the right stuff, he could still make his way to the majors. His high school coach said he had great hand-eye coordination. Greg had six good pitches and could hit at least five.

"Just watch my smoke. I'm not over

the hill yet, man," Greg said.

"Maybe not, but you can sure as heck *see* the hill," Tommy joked.

Just then Greg noticed a man standing at the fence, watching him pitch. The minute Greg made eye contact with him, though, the guy turned away and got into a Camaro parked nearby.

"Hey, Tommy, know what's weird? See that guy in the Camaro? I've seen him watching me before. Lots of times when I'm practicing, he stands over there and looks through the wire fence. Does he look like somebody you know? He looks kinda familiar to me, but I can't place him," Greg said.

"Yeah? Probably it's just some old dude remembering the good old days when he used to throw the baseball around," Tommy said. "Maybe he just likes to watch kids play baseball."

"Maybe. But it makes me feel weird, a guy just standing there staring at me," Greg said, shaking his head. The boys started toward the apartment complex where they both lived. Tommy had left home and now lived with one of his friends, but Greg still lived at home with his parents and two younger brothers.

"Who do you think that guy is?" Tommy asked as they walked.

"You got me," Greg said. "Who knows? Maybe he's a baseball scout who heard about how good I was at Evergreen. He's probably wondering if this youngblood still has the arm."

Tommy punched him playfully. "Dream on, man, dream on," he laughed.

It was awfully crowded in Greg's apartment, but he saved a lot of money living at home. His girlfriend, Julie Ponce, was finishing a cosmetics course at college. Pretty soon after that, Greg and Julie planned to get married.

Greg turned in the direction of his apartment, and Tommy headed down the alley to his place. They worked for the same employer, Beverly Construction.

"Hi, Greg," Mom said when he came in the door. "Have a good day, honey?"

"Yeah, after work I got in some pitching practice with Tommy down at the school," Greg said.

"What for?" his mom asked with a little frown. "That train pulled out of the station a long time ago."

"Sometimes they have open tryouts, Mom. If you're sensational, they send you to a farm club until you can prove you're ready for the majors. In the middle of a season, if a club is hurting for solid pitching, they might call up a kid from the minors," Greg said. He really wasn't *counting on* something like that happening, of course. But he figured it was a better shot than winning the lottery—and his mom was always buying lottery tickets for the big spin.

Grandma was sitting in her favorite chair, sewing. "Oh, don't waste your time on dreams, child. You're a good electrician. That's where your future is.

Do the best job you can there, and you'll always make a good living. It costs a lot to support a family these days. What this world needs is people who understand how to make practical things work," she said.

Greg glanced out the apartment window. He was surprised to see a Camaro parked across the street. He could've sworn it was the same car that was parked at Evergreen High.

"Hey, Mom, some older guy's been watching me pitch at school, and I think he's parked across the street right now," Greg said with excitement. "You figure he's a baseball scout?"

Mom joined Greg at the window. "Honey, I seriously doubt that baseball scouts hang around all day gawking at apartment complexes. If he was interested in talking to you about playing ball, he'd come pounding on the door. Look, he's driving away now. He's probably just some salesman wondering where to go next to peddle his stuff."

"Yeah," Greg agreed, but he couldn't get past the feeling that he knew the guy. His squarish face looked familiar. Even after Greg went to bed, he kept thinking about the man who had lingered at the fence, staring at him.

Then, around eleven, Greg sat bolt upright in bed and yelled, "Vic Hunter! That's the guy! It's *Vic Hunter!*"

"Huh?" mumbled Layne, Greg's 16-year-old brother. "Hey, I'm trying to get some sleep here, man. What're you hollering about, Greg?"

"The guy who's been watching me playing ball at school—the one who parked across the street in the Camaro. I finally figured out who it is. I *knew* I'd seen him before. The guy's name is Vic Hunter. He busted in our house about ten years ago. Remember? Mom and you and Roy came home from the movies and there he was, taking stuff from the dresser!" Greg exclaimed.

His voice was breathless with excitement at recalling the identity of the mysterious stranger.

"You mean that *burglar* is back?" Layne cried, now fully awake.

Chapter 2

"Yeah," Greg said. "You were just six then and Roy was about three. But I was eleven. I remember us all running from the house screaming. That was when the cops caught him. He was convicted for burglary. Seems like he was a real bad guy. He'd been breaking into houses all over town. As I remember, they sent him to prison for a long time. Now he's out and he's shadowing me!"

At breakfast the next morning, Greg told his mom and dad about Vic Hunter. "Mom, you know the guy who's been watching me ... the guy I thought was a baseball scout? Well, I remember who he is now. It's Vic Hunter, that burglar who busted in here ten years ago."

Mom looked shocked. "Are you

sure about that, Greg?" she asked.

"It's him all right," Greg said. "I'm sure of it. I could never forget that face. He was a *notorious* creep—they called him the 'noontime bandit' because he was always coming into people's houses in the middle of the day. His picture was in all the papers and on TV for a long time. It really stuck in my mind."

"Maybe this man just *looks* like Vic Hunter," Mr. Naylor said. "I can't imagine you'd remember him that well after ten years, Greg."

"I'm telling you guys, it's *him*!" Greg said. "I kept some of the news articles about the burglary. I put them away in my scrapbook with pictures we took on vacation in Yosemite and the Grand Canyon. I mean, it was really exciting to an 11-year-old kid that such a famous burglar came to our house. Over the years I've studied his picture whenever I looked at my scrapbook."

Mom looked thoroughly frightened.

"If you see him again, we'll call the police," she said. "We'll get them to write one of those restraining orders to make sure he stays away from us."

"Mom," 13-year-old Roy asked worriedly, "do you think he blames *us* that he got caught? The police nabbed him right after he came here. . . ."

Mom's eyes were wide, swimming in fear. "Maybe. I did give the police the license number of his car. That's how they caught up with him, I guess. I bet he just now got out of prison and he's looking us up!" she said.

Dad put a comforting arm around her shoulder. "Take it easy, honey. Don't worry. He's not gonna bother this family. I'll see to that."

Greg had to leave for work, but he took a few minues to show Layne and Roy his scrapbook with the pictures of Vic Hunter in it. Hunter was ten years younger in the pictures, but from the looks of the man Greg saw yesterday, he hadn't changed much. He'd put on a little more weight, that's all. In the newspaper pictures Vic Hunter had been a slender young man. He had only been 33 when he'd gone off on that crime spree ten years ago.

"Man," Layne said, "he looks really tough."

"You think he came back to get revenge, Greg?" Roy asked.

"I don't know," Greg said, "but let's watch ourselves. Like Mom said, if he shows up again we gotta call the police right away!"

Then Greg drove down to Beverly Construction in his old Toyota pickup truck. He and Tommy carpooled. Every other day they drove to work in Tommy's Chevy.

All day Greg worked hard putting wiring in a tract of new houses on the west side. Then, after work, he took Tommy home and went to visit his girlfriend. Julie rented a room in a boarding house about three miles from Greg's apartment.

"It'll be cool when we have our own place," Julie said. "I'm so tired of this cramped little room and the landlady always messing with my stuff. This house is so full of people all the time that I can't even sleep!"

Greg was looking forward to that, too. The apartment where his family lived was nice enough, but it sure wasn't roomy—not with Mom, Dad, Grandma, and three boys living there. Mom had married Greg's stepfather when Greg was just a baby. To Greg, the man was *Dad*, no question about it. Ham Naylor was a security guard, and he didn't make great money. But he was a wonderful father to the three boys. Greg wouldn't ever have traded his stepdad for any other guy's "real" father.

Greg didn't spend any time at all wondering about his biological father. Mom just said he was a kid and she was a kid—and when a child was on the way, the guy had cut out fast. Grandma and Mom raised Greg until Ham Naylor came along. Ham and Greg both grinned when friends would say that Greg, of all the three boys, was the most like his father. It was true. Greg had grown up adoring Ham Naylor and trying to be like him in every way possible.

"Julie, let's get out of here and go for a burger," Greg said.

"Yeah, with fries," Julie smiled.

"Julie, you know that guy who's been shadowing me?" Greg said.

"Yeah, the baseball scout," she said.

"Turns out he's no baseball scout," Greg said. "Turns out he's a criminal. Ten years ago he burglarized our house. Now we're afraid he's out of jail and looking for revenge. After all, Mom was the one who got him busted!"

Chapter 3

"Are you *sure*, Greg? That's awful!" Julie cried. "If that's the case, you'd better be careful!"

"Yeah. This guy was dubbed the 'noontime bandit' ten years ago because that's when he'd hit houses. He was especially dangerous because he'd come right in when people were at home. The cops call it a 'hot prowl' when a guy comes in an occupied house to steal," Greg explained.

"Better watch yourself. I've heard of guys coming out of prison even more vicious than when they went in. If you see him, call the police," Julie said.

"I know, I know. That's what Mom says too," Greg said.

At work the next day, one of the

other electricians, a guy named Adam Lewis, was goofing off as usual instead of working on the electrical outlets in the model home.

Greg didn't like Lewis. The guy dragged the whole crew down. He was always sneaking off the job to grab a cigarette. That really annoyed Greg—not because Greg was a stooge for the boss, Mr. Beverly—but because it made everybody look bad. If a job was messed up, *all* the electricians would be blamed. Greg was trying hard to build a first-rate reputation. This was his first full-time job. He was counting on a good reference from Beverly Construction.

Now, Lewis was about to go outside for his second cigarette in an hour. Greg looked at him and said, "Hey, Lewis, we got to get this done before one o'clock, you know. The city inspector is coming then. If we're not finished, he has to come back another time, and that delays the whole job."

Adam Lewis was about 30, and he thought he was the *man*. He was a wisecracking, handsome dude who enjoyed dissing the boss. So he didn't take kindly to a young guy Greg's age taking him to task. "Just mind your own business, junior. I was installing electrical outlets when you were a failing kidlet in fifth grade. So keep your nose out of my business and bug off, okay?" Lewis snapped.

"Look, Lewis, we're behind schedule because one guy—you—takes way too many breaks. You're slowing down the whole crew, and you know it. I don't want to look bad because you don't care about your work," Greg said.

"Don't get in my face, Naylor, understand? The last guy who did that ended up in the ER with a busted jaw," Lewis growled, pulling out a cigarette and walking off.

Greg shook his head in disgust. Mr. Beverly didn't run a very tight ship. He should have been on the job more, finding out for himself who was working hard and who was dragging his tail. The last time the city inspectors came, they found 12 violations of code on the electrical work done. *All* of it was Lewis's work. If that continued to happen, Beverly Construction was in trouble. They could easily lose the big job they had just landed.

Early that afternoon, Mr. Beverly came in to check on the progress of the electricians and plumbers. He saw several beer cans and a pile of cigarette stubs in the trash.

"Listen, you guys," Beverly said gruffly, "knock off the beer drinking on the job! And there's too many cigarette breaks around here. I know a cold beer tastes good when it's hot out, but do it on your own time, not mine."

"Yeah, Naylor," Lewis said, "stop swilling so much beer, kid." He sneered at Greg as he said it.

Greg looked up sharply. He wasn't a snitch, but he wasn't a fool, either. "I don't drink beer," he snapped.

"Well, I don't know *who's* been drinking on the job—but I don't want anymore of it," Beverly said. "If I catch anybody drinking before quitting time, that's *it*! He can get his pay and clear out right then and there. And I'm not kidding, either." With that the old man glared at everyone and stomped off.

Greg stared at Lewis. "I don't much like you making stupid cracks like that to the boss," he said.

Lewis laughed. "Lighten up, kid. The old man is just blowing off steam. Don't worry. He's not about to fire anybody. He's just a big bag of hot air."

"Well, don't say ridiculous things like that to him anymore," Greg said.

Adam Lewis was a big man, at least 220 pounds, with a big bull neck and arms bulging with muscles. Greg was tall and rangy—a poor match for Lewis

23

if it ever came down to that.

"Ooooo, I'm really nervous when you talk tough to me like that, Naylor," Lewis said mockingly. "I'm scared to death you're gonna beat me up or something. *Get real*, kid. I'll do what I want when I want. Nobody is giving me orders—not the old man and for sure not a little punk like you."

Oh, great, Greg thought. He needed an enemy on the job like he needed another hole in his head. He had a good job and he was saving as much as he could for his life with Julie. Greg had collected a lot of praise from Mr. Beverly for his good work. He could imagine himself moving up fast in this company. Mr. Beverly's son was a partner, so the company would go on and grow even bigger when the old man retired. And Greg had earned top grades in all his construction classes. He felt very good about the quality of his work. A jerk like Adam Lewis could threaten everything.

And as if that wasn't bad enough, now a creepy ex-con was shadowing him. Maybe the guy really *did* want to take vengeance for something that had happened ten years ago!

How could everything have gone so wrong so fast?

Greg worked hard all afternoon and tried to ignore Lewis' jibes. But Lewis was really on Greg's case now, taking every opportunity to hassle him.

"Hey, Naylor, you sure you slid that wire in right? It looks kinda cockeyed to me," he called out.

Greg said nothing and kept on working. He was sorry now he had said anything at all to Lewis. It had just made matters worse.

When Greg finally got off work, he was in a bad mood. He couldn't stand anymore hassle from anybody else. So when Greg and Tommy got over to the Evergreen High playing field to pitch a few balls, the last person he wanted to see was the guy in the Camaro.

This time, Greg strode right up to the car as the man was getting out. "Hey, man, what's coming down?" Greg barked, making himself sound as tough as he could.

The man looked startled. "I'm not sure what you mean," he said, smiling nervously. He wasn't at all what Greg had expected. He wasn't acting like some hate-filled monster with vengeance on his mind. But then convicts were good at conning other people. Maybe he was just playing it cool.

"Look, man," Greg said, "I know who you are. You're Vic Hunter—the old noontime bandit. I guess you know who I am, too."

Hunter nodded, "I do. You're Darla Naylor's boy," he said.

"That's right. So what are you doing hanging around here? We're going to the cops to get a restraining order against you, man. My family is sick and tired of seeing your face, so bug off. . . ."

"I just like watching kids play baseball," Vic Hunter said meekly. Greg thought he sounded *too* wimpy. Surely a man who had broken into all those homes and businesses couldn't be so easily cowed by a young guy like Greg! Vic Hunter's rap sheet went way back to when he was 14 years old. The man had more than a decade of serious prison time under his belt.

What was his game? Maybe right now he was playing possum. Maybe he was just waiting for the perfect chance to strike out!

Chapter 4

"You like baseball, huh? Well, go watch somewhere else," Greg said. "I don't want you hanging around here. And I don't want to see you at our apartment, either. I swear it, man—we're calling the cops on you if you show up again. You can bet they'll put you back in the slammer so fast it'll make your head spin."

Vic Hunter didn't say another word. He simply got back in his car and drove off down the street.

Just after Hunter pulled away, Tommy came walking up. "Hey, man, did you find out if he was a baseball scout?"

Greg laughed bitterly. "Nah. He's an ex-con who actually broke into our apartment ten years ago. Must have just got out of prison. He was pretty famous back then. The cops couldn't nab him until my mom gave them his license number," he said.

"What's he dogging you for?" Tommy asked. "He looking to settle a score?"

"Who knows?" Greg said. "Come on, hotshot, let's play some ball."

The boys played until dark and then packed up their gear. Since the high school playing field was just a couple of blocks from home, Greg and Tommy usually jogged there. But today Greg jogged toward home alone while Tommy headed off in another direction to visit a cousin.

Then, suddenly, as Greg ran down the street, a car pulled up alongside him. There were four guys inside, and they all looked drunk. One of the passengers was Adam Lewis.

"Hey, chump!" Lewis yelled out at Greg. "What's your hurry—you rob a deli? Is that why you're running?"

Greg ignored him. He hoped the weaving car would get the boys stopped by the police.

"Just look at that skinny little runt," Lewis taunted. "He calls himself an electrician, but he can't tell an inductor from a capacitor!"

Greg turned into a convenience store. He phoned the police and told them there were several drunken guys in a car that was driving erratically on Poplar Street. Then he bought a can of soda and came back outside. Lewis and his friends were still cruising along. When they saw Greg, they made a U-turn in the middle of the street and came back.

"Why don't you have a beer like a *real* man, Naylor?" Lewis shouted. "How come you're drinking kiddie pop?"

Greg pulled the tab on the soda can and began drinking as he walked down the street. He ignored the jeers and taunts from Lewis until an empty crunched-up beer can came flying at him. It didn't do any damage. But it made Greg mad, so he spun around and yelled, "Knock it off, you jerk!"

Just then a police car came up Poplar Street. Spotting the weaving car, the officer drove up behind Lewis and his friends, his red light blinking.

"Oh, man," the driver of the car groaned. "We're busted!" He wasn't fool enough to take off and lead the police on a chase, but he knew he was in deep trouble. He was at about twice the legal limit for blood alcohol. Now he was looking at a DUI for sure.

Greg stood there for a few minutes, watching the show. He watched the driver go through the sobriety test. The guy couldn't walk a straight line to save his life. And he sure as heck couldn't beat the breath test.

Adam Lewis' gaze locked on Greg for a minute. The hatred in his face said, *"You did this. You called the cops, didn't you, you little punk?"* Drunk as he was, he had put two and two together. Now he figured he knew why Greg had gone into the convenience store.

Greg turned and walked on home. Unfortunately, Adam Lewis himself wasn't in trouble. He'd just have to walk home. There was no law against being drunk in a car if you weren't driving. But Lewis' buddy was already in the police car.

When Greg got home, he told his mother about the confrontation with Vic Hunter. "I told him to stay away from us, Mom, and he really seemed to get the message."

Mom looked startled. "You actually *talked* to him?" she asked.

"Yeah. I think prison must have broken the guy, Mom. He doesn't seem to have enough fight in him to cause us any trouble. I don't think he'll bother us again," Greg said with pride.

"But what did he say?" Mom asked.

"Almost nothing," Greg said.

"But he must have said *something*," Mom asked, her eyes wide with concern. "Did he say why he was watching you?"

"He just said he likes to see kids play baseball," Greg laughed. "Don't sweat it, Mom. Now that I met him, I'm not afraid of him anymore. He slunk off like a dog with his tail between his legs."

"Don't be so sure, Greg. You don't really *know* him," Mom warned.

"You don't either, Mom. Like we came home that day and here was this burglar in our house. But how much do you actually *know* about him?" Greg countered.

"I know that he was terrorizing the city for months, breaking into all those houses and businesses. He's a very dangerous man. Anyone who would go into a private home to steal is a dangerous criminal," Mom said. "Greg, don't *ever* talk to him again. Who knows what he might do! I don't want you going *near* him! If you see him again, just call the police, okay?"

"Yeah, sure, Mom," Greg said. Then he went up on the roof of the building for some weightlifting. He liked to lift weights up there. With nothing but privacy all around and the starry sky above, it was like having his own big, private gym.

The next day at work, Greg kept getting hate looks from Adam Lewis. But Lewis didn't come anywhere near him. Maybe that was because Mr. Beverly was on the job site all day. The old man was lurking around, looking over everybody's shoulder, watching them work. Greg didn't mind. He was proud of the work he was doing, and he was glad the old man was taking notice. And with the boss around, Lewis didn't get so many chances to sneak out for his beer and cigarette breaks.

For the next few days, Greg didn't see the Camaro around. But he had the strange feeling that he was being watched, anyway. He couldn't explain the feeling, but it was there. Maybe it was just his imagination, but he'd be walking down the street and suddenly get a creepy feeling that somebody's eyes were trained on him.

He wondered if Vic Hunter had taken a room in one of those cheap hotels with a view of the apartments where Greg and his family lived. From some of those hotel rooms you could see the whole street. If you had binoculars, you could even see all the way over to Evergreen High School.

Maybe Vic Hunter was sitting behind one of those dirty windows with the torn curtains. Maybe he was there now, peering through a pair of binoculars, marking Greg's comings and goings.

But *why*? When Greg asked himself that question, he always came up with the same answer. The guy had a grudge. He was biding his time, just waiting for the perfect opportunity to take revenge on the woman who had sent him up the river—and on her family as well.

Then, suddenly, Greg wondered if *this* wasn't the revenge—or at least part of it. Maybe just lurking out there in the shadows, knowing he was making his victims nervous, was the man's way of getting even until he could think of something worse. It was certainly putting everybody's nerves on edge. It could be that all those years of sitting in a grim prison cell had prepared him to wait patiently for his chance and to torment his prey before striking. Maybe he wanted to drive the Naylors a little crazy before he moved in for the kill.

The strategy sure seemed to be working with Mom. Last night, when someone had accidentally slammed a door, she dropped the meatloaf she was lifting from the oven. And tonight she had burned the pork chops.

Chapter 5

Yeah, Greg thought, such a sneaky kind of revenge might very well fit the character of Vic Hunter. He was a weasel—a nasty little creeper who broke into people's homes and rummaged through their private stuff, putting his dirty paws on their precious belongings. What kind of man was that?

Greg had read quite a bit about the man in the newspapers. In all his criminal life, Hunter never carried a weapon. He wasn't violent. He'd never even gotten into a fight with a victim. One of his victims, a 75-year-old woman, had come home to find him in her kitchen, and chased him out wielding only a can opener.

But Mom's call got him sent up. He

was mad about that. That's how Greg saw it. Mom's call got him ten long years in the slammer—and you don't forget the person who did that to you! So he was exacting his revenge in his own way. He was going to be the gnat flying around their heads, the one they couldn't catch. Nothing could be more maddening than a pesky gnat, the one that seemed to be gone at last, only to reappear, buzzing in your ear the minute you sat down.

Greg had figured out Hunter's game. The man was going to be the shadow, the sinister shadow that remained behind you so that you couldn't see him make his move. But who could tell what might happen? Maybe, for the first time in his life, Hunter would get violent. After all, ten years in prison had to be pretty hard to take. Maybe it had pushed him over the edge.

When the electricians showed up at Beverly Construction the next day, the old man introduced a new member of the team, Pedro Torrez.

"Hey, we weren't short a guy," the man next to Greg muttered.

"Yesterday afternoon I fired Adam Lewis," Mr. Beverly said matter-of-factly. "The man wasn't cutting the mustard, and he had a bad attitude to boot."

Greg was glad that Lewis was gone. Apparently Mr. Beverly had picked up enough about him yesterday to see that he was loafing on the job. Everybody there knew it. Adam Lewis was always dragging his feet, slowing things down, joking and horsing around. Greg figured some of the other guys had probably ratted on Lewis, too. The guy wasn't liked by anybody.

After work, Greg was whistling as he went to his pickup for the ride home. Tommy was going home with another construction worker. The guy was going to introduce Tommy to his pretty sister. Greg planned to pick Julie up, and then head out for dinner and the movies. He was feeling pretty good right now.

Later, when Greg and Julie were eating their chicken enchiladas, Greg told her about Lewis getting fired. "I'm so glad that jerk is out of there," Greg said. "He was making me look bad. He was ruining it for all the guys."

"How did he take being fired?" Julie asked.

"I don't know. Beverly did it last night after we were all gone. I suppose Lewis is gonna think I snitched on him, but I didn't. I bet some of the other guys did, though. But even if nobody said anything against him, Beverly was bound to figure it out sooner or later. Lewis was no good," Greg said.

After dinner, Greg and Julie got in the pickup and drove toward the movie in the mall. Then as they parked and started walking toward the theater, Adam Lewis and his buddy appeared out of nowhere. Apparently they had been following Greg and Julie, but Greg hadn't seen them in the darkness.

"You ratted on me, Naylor," Lewis snarled. "You talked the old geezer into canning me. And you called the cops on Ric, too. Now he's sitting in jail on a DUI charge, and he's gonna lose his truck driving job."

Greg looked at Lewis and his buddy. They were both built like tanks. They weren't drunk, but clearly they had both been drinking. Alcohol had made them meaner and more dangerous than ever.

"Look, Lewis, I never said anything against you on the job. Old man Beverly must have figured it all out without any help from me."

Greg was nervous about being here with Julie. If trouble started, Julie could get hurt. He wished there were some people around, but the parking garage was pretty deserted at this time of night.

"*Liar!*" Lewis said. "You got me canned. Who do you think you are to mess with me and my friends?"

"Look, man, this mall has security guards all over the place. In about two minutes they're gonna come around—so why don't you and your friend there just move along now," Greg said.

"Listen, you guys," Julie said. "If I start screaming, they'll be able to hear me in the next county. We don't want any trouble, so just get lost."

The two big men backed off, but Lewis was still seething with rage. "There'll be another time, *chump*!" he threatened.

Greg took Julie's hand and they hurried across the street to the theater. When Greg looked back, he saw that Lewis and the other guy were staring after them, seething in frustration.

"Julie," Greg said, "you go inside the movie theater. I'm doubling back so I can move my truck. Those jerks know where we're parked. I don't want them tampering with my truck."

"Greg! I don't want you going back inside that dark parking garage alone!" Julie argued.

"Don't worry, honey. I'll make sure they're gone before I go near the truck. If they're still there, I'll get a security guard to go with me. Just go on in the movie and buy me a bag of popcorn, too. As soon as I park the truck in another place, I'll join you," Greg said.

Greg hurried from the theater lobby and looked across the street. As far as he could see, the guys were gone. So he dashed into the parking garage, watching his back as he went. When he reached his truck, he breathed a sigh of relief. It wasn't keyed, and no holes were punched in the tires. Everything was okay so far. Greg's pickup was painted a metallic blue with some silver lightning bolts on the sides. He was proud of how good his old truck looked.

Greg drove around to the other side of the theater, and parked in a well-lighted lot near an all-night burger joint. Then he hurried back to the theater to join Julie. He headed for the row where they always sat. But all the seats in that row were empty. *Julie wasn't there!*

Greg broke out in a cold sweat. He told himself she must have gone to the restroom. But after hanging around for a few minutes, he got the usher.

"Look, my girlfriend is supposed to be here, but now I can't find her. She was going to wait for me here with a couple of bags of popcorn. Would somebody go check the ladies' room? She's got dark hair and she's wearing a red pullover and jeans. I'm worried, because some guys were hassling us out in the parking garage," Greg said nervously.

The ushers searched the theater with flashlights and one of the girl ushers checked the restroom.

"Sorry, sir," the head usher said. "Your friend just isn't here."

Greg felt a surge of panic, but he

tried to stay calm. Julie was probably so worried about him going to the parking garage alone that she followed him. That would be just like her. But when she found the pickup moved, how was she to know that everything was cool? Maybe she was still looking for him, wandering around out there. . . .

And maybe Lewis and his pal were still out there, too!

Greg started to breathe hard. A swarm of fears attacked him like nasty wasps. Had those two thugs waylaid Julie when she came out to check on Greg? It chilled Greg's bones to imagine what those two might do to Julie if they got her down some dark alley. Lewis would really relish getting that kind of revenge on Greg!

Greg ran through the whole parking garage shouting Julie's name. "Julie! Julie!" he yelled again and again.

Hearing all the ruckus, an elderly man came shuffling over, pushing a wire shopping cart filled with all his worldly possessions. Even here, at this pricey mall, there were plenty of these unfortunate people—the homeless.

"Who you hollering for, son?" the old man asked in a friendly voice.

"My girlfriend. I left her in the movie theater and now she's gone," Greg said.

"Ah, ditched you, huh?" he said sympathetically. "They'll do it every time. I had me a real pretty little girl once . . . Naomi was her name. Was right after the war," the man rambled on.

"I got no time for this," Greg said. He continued to shout Julie's name.

"She wearing a red sweater?" the homeless man asked.

Greg spun around. "Yeah, man! Tell me—what do you know about her? Where did she go? Man, you gotta tell me what happened to her!"

"Well, this fella was helping her into his car. I figured they were together and she got sick is all. Looked like they were on a date and maybe she had too much to drink. Lotsa young folks drink too much these days. Now, Naomi, she never touched a drop—but she was flighty," the man said.

"What did the guy who took her look like? What kind of a car did he have?" Greg demanded, desperately gripping the man's coat.

He knew that Adam Lewis drove an old Mazda.

"Ahh, I didn't see the fella real good. He just sorta lifted her in the car and closed the door and off they went," the homeless man said, shrugging.

"What kind of a car?" Greg repeated.

"Ahh, yeah, it was the kind of car I always wanted. I had me a Pinto and a Rambler, but they weren't the kind I wanted . . . I never had a Camaro and that's the one I wanted," the man said with a smile.

"Oh, no! She went off in a *Camaro*?" Greg gasped.

"Yeah, it was one of them Camaros, all right. An *old* Camaro—but she was still a beaut, yessiree," the man said, still smiling, lost in his memories.

Greg felt sick to his stomach. He had assumed that Julie was grabbed by Adam Lewis and his friend. But now it seemed that Hunter had been following Greg again! He must have trailed him to the parking garage and then on to the lot near the burger joint.

The man seemed like a *devil* who just wouldn't go away. Hunter, looking for a way to get revenge. Hunter, patiently waiting for his chance.

And now he had Julie!

# Chapter 6

Greg rushed to a telephone to call his mother. Once he told her that Vic Hunter had apparently kidnapped Julie, Mom could call the police while he tried to track them down. If Greg hurried, maybe he could pick up the Camaro's trail out on the streets.

"Mom," Greg shouted into the phone, "something's happened to Julie!"

Mom cut in before he could give her details. "Yes, I know, Greg. Listen to me. Julie just called from the ER. Don't worry—she's fine. She's being treated for an eye irritation. An unknown assailant sprayed something in her face while she was looking for you in the mall parking area. You've got to go down to South End Hospital and pick her up. She's going to be released in a few minutes."

"But ... but ... how did she get to the hospital?" Greg asked.

"I don't know, Greg. She was very upset when she called here. I couldn't make sense out of what she was saying. She said she was looking for you when she suddenly felt a burning spray of some kind hit her face. She said her eyes were very painful, and that she was terrified that she'd been blinded. She remembered screaming for help, and then somebody came along and took her to the hospital, I guess. Go get her *now*, Greg. I don't want her parents finding out that she's in the hospital and getting all frantic," Mom said.

Greg ran to the pickup truck and took off for the hospital. He was *so* relieved that Julie was all right! But he was also very confused.

The admitting nurse in the ER led Greg through some doors into the examination area. He spotted Julie, now fully dressed, sitting on the edge of a bed.

"Oh, Greg!" Julie cried when she saw him. "I'm so glad to see you!"

"Babe, what happened?" Greg asked, putting his arms around her.

"I'm not sure. I got so worried about you going back into that dark parking garage . . . I thought Lewis and his friend might jump you and beat you up and leave you unconscious. So I left the theater and walked into the garage. When I got near where you had parked the truck, I heard this guy laughing like a maniac. Then, the next thing I knew, this horrible spray hit me in the face, and I couldn't see a thing.

"It was terrible, Greg. It hurt so much, and I almost died of fright! I started stumbling around and crying, and then some man came along and helped me wash out my eyes . . . and he took me to the hospital in his car," Julie explained.

"Do you think the guy who sprayed you might have been the guy who took you to the hospital?" Greg asked.

"Come on, Greg—that doesn't make any sense," Julie said.

But maybe it did. Maybe Vic Hunter just wanted to let the Naylors know how vulnerable they really were. Perhaps he wanted to show them that he was always right there, and could do what he wanted, whenever he wanted. Probably that was step two of his vengeance program.

Greg was sick with fear and worry. "Julie, what did this guy say when he drove you to the hospital?" he asked.

"Nothing much. Just things like, 'We're almost there' and stuff like that. He seemed like a very nice man, a real Good Samaritan," Julie remembered.

"Did the doctor say your eyes are okay, Julie?" Greg asked anxiously.

"Yes—my vision wasn't damaged, thank heaven! But oh, Greg, I've never been so scared in my entire life! Do you think that Adam Lewis who got fired at your job could be the one who did it?" Julie asked.

"I don't know," Greg said.

Greg drove Julie home, and they sat in the pickup for a few minutes before she went in. "Julie, somebody's got my number. You better stay away from me until I find out what's coming down. I don't want you getting hurt anymore, okay? Some bad guy is trying to hurt me and my family by hurting *you*. Until I can find out who it is, you're better off keeping your distance," Greg said.

Julie grabbed Greg's arm. "I'm *not* going to stay away from you. *I love you!* You think I'm the kind of person who jumps ship when the going gets rough? Not me! I'm in this relationship for the long haul, Greg."

Greg leaned over and kissed her. He was so relieved that she was all right! They sat in the pickup for a good ten minutes, just holding each other. Then Julie went inside and Greg headed home.

His brain was spinning. What if Adam Lewis and his buddy had kidnapped Julie and roughed her up to get even with Greg? They might've sprayed her with some pepper spray. Then maybe some other guy came along and scared them off. But why would Vic Hunter rescue Julie? Julie was right—it *didn't* make any sense. Hunter was a career criminal, after all. Surely he wasn't the sort of a guy who stopped to help people in distress.

But just *maybe*, Greg thought, Hunter did spray Julie and then rushed her to the hospital. Maybe his only desire was to terrorize someone Greg loved—to put him through the hell of not knowing where his girlfriend was. Maybe he had spent all those bitter years in prison hatching diabolical stunts like this, plans he couldn't wait to carry out when he finally got the chance.

Chapter 7

For an hour or so, Greg cruised around the neighborhood, looking for the Camaro and Lewis' Mazda. He was seething with rage about what had been done to Julie. If he found out who did it, he'd drag him out of his car and beat the truth out of him! But Greg never saw either car, so he finally went home.

In the morning there was a strange envelope in the Naylor mail slot. It didn't have a name or address on it. Whoever had left it must have come to the door to put it in. The envelope bore no stamp, so it hadn't come through the mail.

The message inside had been written by cutting out letters from magazine and newspaper ads and pasting them down. It was very brief:

"The worst is yet to come."

It was signed, also in cut-out letters, *"The Avenger."*

"Mom!" Greg shouted.

"I'm only in the kitchen," Mom said, "you don't have to scream."

Greg immediately showed the note to his mother and brothers.

"Oh, man!" Layne cried. "It must be that guy—Vic Hunter, huh?"

"Let's call the cops now," Roy said. "They'll put out an all-points bulletin and close in on him."

"Do *you* think Hunter left this note, Mom?" Greg asked.

Mom had a strange look on her face. He had never seen her so agitated and sad looking. "No," she said.

"But he *must* have done it, Mom," Roy insisted. "He's a real criminal. He hates us 'cause you were the one got him arrested and sent off to prison for ten years. It even says so in a news story Greg has. It says, 'Alert woman traps noontime bandit' and it tells about *you*, Mom!"

"Yeah," Layne said, "he's out to get us, for sure. We *gotta* call the cops."

Mom sat down and closed her eyes. "Maybe so," she admitted. "This is all hard to believe, but maybe we should." She looked at Greg. "What if it's that guy from your job—that Lewis guy? You said he was mean and vindictive. And he blames you for getting him fired. Don't you think we have to be *sure* before we start pointing a finger at someone?"

"Yeah," Greg agreed. "It wouldn't be right to sic the cops on Hunter if he's not the guy who's after us."

That evening, Greg did what he often did to relax—he went up on the roof to lift weights. He wanted big muscles, and he was following the bodybuilding program he had learned in his wrestling classes at high school. He wanted to be able to deal with bullies like Adam

Lewis if he ever had to. Besides, it just made him feel good to lift weights.

A beautiful red sunset was visible from the roof that evening, and Greg just stood there for a few minutes, drinking in the sight. In less than an hour, darkness would cover the city. Then hundreds of streetlights would compete with the stars.

Greg worked out for an hour and then stopped for a long gulp of water. He thought he'd call Julie when he went back downstairs. Maybe they could rent a movie and get takeout pizza. It would give them something better to think about than the mysterious, ugly things that had been happening.

Turning around in the dim light, he was heading for the stairs when he saw two hulking shapes coming toward him.

"Hey there, chump," Adam Lewis snarled. "This is Ric, the guy you got busted for DUI. Today Ric got fired just like me. So you ruined it for both of us, right? Well, you ain't getting away with it, punk. You better pray that all that weightlifting has been doing you some good. *It's payback time.*"

Chapter 8

Greg's jaw dropped. Ric was even bigger and tougher looking than Lewis. "A snitch is the worst kind of lowlife in the world," Ric growled.

Adam Lewis took a transistor radio from his backpack. Then he tuned in to a rap music station and cranked up the volume. "We wouldn't want anybody getting upset by strange noises. You know, man—like screams," Lewis said with an evil smile.

Greg moved backward slowly. He thought maybe he could make an end run toward the stairs and race down ahead of them. He couldn't take on these guys, pound for pound, but he could at least run faster. As it turned out, however, he wasn't quite fast enough.

The second he sprang into motion, the two of them came lunging at him, throwing him down.

"You shouldn't have told Beverly to can me, man," Lewis grunted. "That was a bad mistake."

"Snitches are nothing but *scum*," Ric hissed, *"pond* scum."

"I didn't say anything to Beverly," Greg said, but he knew that wouldn't convince Lewis of anything.

It was full dusk now. Yet still, if somebody happened to be looking up at the apartment roof, they would see two guys getting the best of a third guy. But who was watching? Everybody was inside their apartments at this hour, watching TV or eating dinner.

Nobody was staring up at the roof of this old apartment, Greg figured. These thugs could beat him to a pulp, and not a soul would notice.

But that wasn't what the pair had in mind. Their breaths smelled of liquor and their eyes were bloodshot. Sober, they might have balked at murder. But they'd drunk a lot of courage tonight, adding fuel to their madness. They weren't thinking clearly anymore.

"You're going over the edge, man," Lewis said. "You're going down five stories, and you're gonna smash like a big old watermelon on the concrete below." Then Lewis laughed like a maniac, and Greg remembered what Julie had said. *The guy who sprayed her in the face had laughed like that.*

So it was Lewis. Greg knew that now—too late.

Lewis held Greg on one side and Ric held him on the other. They began dragging him toward the edge of the roof. If Greg screamed for help, the yell would be drowned out by the rap music. Even if the tenants down below heard a scream, they wouldn't *do* anything. This was the kind of neighborhood where people screamed a lot, for a lot of reasons. And most of the time people minded their own business.

Lewis and Ric dragged Greg closer to the edge. To slow them down, Greg tried to relax and make himself dead weight. They continued to drag him closer to the edge anyway.

"You won't ever rat on anybody again, man," Ric gloated.

"You guys are crazy," Greg said. "You'll burn for murder."

"Nah," Lewis said. "It'll just look like a real bad accident. Another crazy guy falling off a roof."

"Look, you won't get away with this," Greg said. "You'll get caught and you'll rot in prison for the rest of your lives—if they don't burn you."

"Save your breath. You're going over the edge, man," Lewis snarled. "Believe it, punk, you're gonna *pay!*"

Greg jerked with all his might, kicking at his captors. That slowed them down a bit, but he was still being steadily dragged to the edge of the roof.

"When you hit the cement, you'll weigh a lot more than you do now, man," Lewis snickered. "Didn't we learn that in high school math—a falling object gets heavier as it goes down?" Then he laughed again, insanely, like a maniac.

"Anyone who ever watched a cartoon knows what will happen, man. You'll go *splat*!" Ric laughed.

Greg heard the roar of traffic on the street below. Then he closed his eyes and went numb.

Chapter 9

Then Greg heard something else—an *incredible* sound! It was a helicopter growling overhead, its brilliant lights bathing the roof of the apartment building. A stern voice blasted from the helicopter's sound system. *"You men on the roof—don't move. This is the police."*

Greg tingled with relief. He couldn't believe what was happening. He had been only a few feet from death, and now police officers were streaming toward him from the stairs while the helicopter hovered overhead.

"They were gonna throw me over," Greg gasped.

"That's sure what it looked like," one of the police officers said.

"Man, I thought I was doomed!"

Greg cried. "How did you get here?"

The cop smiled and shrugged. "Some fella in the hotel across the street was looking over here with binoculars. I guess he's some kind of eccentric who likes to spy on his neighbors. But it's a good thing he was looking *this* time! He called us and said that two guys were trying to kill another guy and we should get here fast. He seemed real excited."

Lewis and Ric were taken away in handcuffs. In Greg's statement to the police, he explained about being blamed for losing their jobs. Then, exhausted, he climbed back downstairs to his apartment. Mom threw her arms around him. "Oh, baby, thank God you're all right!" she cried.

The Naylors had only discovered what was going on when the police came flooding into the building.

Greg looked hard at his mother. "Mom, that guy, Vic Hunter. For a while now I've had this spooky feeling that he was watching me from one of the hotels across the street. The cop said a guy in the hotel tipped them to come help me. I think it was Hunter...and I think Hunter helped Julie the other night—because he was following us. Now he saved *my* life...what's going on, Mom?"

Greg's mother had tears in her eyes. She walked into the living room and asked Greg to come sit beside her. Then she reached over and grasped Greg's hand. "Darling, your dad loves you more than anybody ever loved a boy. That's a big reason why he works so hard. He was in the hospital when you were born and he loves you," Mom said.

"Yeah, I know that, Mom," Greg said, wondering what her point was.

Nobody needed to tell Greg that Ham Naylor was a great dad. The man worked 18 hours a day sometimes, just to give his family a good life. Greg thought the world of him.

"Greg, you know I was already

expecting you when I married your dad," Mom went on.

"Sure, Mom," Greg said impatiently. "So?"

"The boy I married as a teenager, my first love . . . *your father* . . . He was a thief and a burglar. I didn't know it at the time, but he had always been a criminal. Yet in spite of that he was a sweet and charming fellow. Greg . . . *Vic Hunter is your biological father*," Mom said.

Greg felt as if the wind had been knocked out of him. "But. . . but . . . he broke into our apartment to rob us!" he gasped in confusion.

"He *was* the noontime bandit, yes. But that day he broke in for another reason. He had come here to see his son. I knew that, and it frightened me. I was frightened for *you*. So I decided to turn him in anyway. I gave the police all the information they needed to catch him and put him away. He led a bad life—

and I was trying to protect you. I couldn't bear to have an out-and-out criminal play any part in my child's life," Mom said.

Chapter 10

Greg couldn't believe what he was hearing. "Does Dad know?" Greg asked.

"Yes, he's always known," Mom said.

Greg was silent for a moment, but then he asked, "Why didn't Hunter tell me the truth when I confronted him that day?"

A fresh burst of tears trickled down Mom's face. "I guess in his own twisted way he loves you, too. He didn't want to mess up your family life with the horrible truth," she said.

Greg got up slowly. He leaned down and kissed his mother, and then went downstairs and out into the darkness. He crossed the street and went into the cheap hotel that offered the best view of the Naylors' apartment windows and the roof of the building where they lived.

When Greg described the man to the desk clerk, he knew just who Greg was talking about. He told him that Vic Hunter was in Room 6D, registered under the name of Joe Johnson.

Greg rapped on the door, and in a few minutes Vic Hunter appeared.

"I saw you coming," Hunter said nervously, binoculars in hand.

"You're the one who saw the fight, too, huh?" Greg asked.

"Yes—I was really scared," Hunter said. "You want to come in? It's not very fancy, but—"

"Yeah," Greg said, choosing one of the lumpy chairs. "Thanks for what you did for my girlfriend Julie the other night. And . . . thanks for saving my life. Those guys were out to kill me."

"I was really afraid of that," Hunter said. "They looked mean. And believe me, I can tell a mean soul when I see one. I met plenty of them in prison. But not all the men in prison are like that."

"Mom told me everything," Greg said quietly.

Hunter paled. *"Everything?"*

"Yeah," Greg said.

Hunter clasped his shaking hands and looked down for a few moments. Then he looked up at Greg. "You know, I am a very bad man. I've been a thief since I was 14 years old. I've spent half my adult life in prison. I loved your mom, but I was too lazy and irresponsible to work. Stealing was easier. When she was expecting you, I ran away. I've done nothing in my life that I'm proud of."

Greg saw the pain in the man's face as he went on. "The word *nothing* just about tells it all, I'm afraid. I've had no love, no family, and no joy in my life. I don't deserve any. The only thing I ever did that turned out good was you. I'm proud of you, Greg. You're such a handsome, fine boy. I just wanted to check in on you, to make sure that you were doing all right.

"Just looking at you from a distance—why, it gave me the only happiness I've ever had. I know I didn't raise a finger to help bring you up, and I don't even deserve a handshake from you. But just to know you *are* gave me a reason to get up in the morning. . . ." Hunter said in a hoarse whisper.

Greg stood up. He cleared his throat a few times. "Hey, if you want to come over to Evergreen and see me pitch sometime . . . it'd be okay," he said.

"Yeah?" Hunter said. "Honest?"

"Sure," Greg said, "and we might even get some hotdogs afterward . . . or some soda, you know, like that. . . ."

"I like hotdogs," Vic Hunter said in a shaky voice.

COMPREHENSION QUESTIONS

RECALL

1. What work did Greg Naylor do for a living? What work would he *rather* have been doing?

2. What kind of car did Vic Hunter drive?

3. Where was Greg when Adam and Ric attacked him? What was he doing there?

CAUSE AND EFFECT

1. Greg scolded Adam Lewis for goofing off and making all the electricians look bad. What was the *effect* of that scolding?

2. Mrs. Naylor gave the police Vic Hunter's license plate number. What was the *effect* of her action?

3. What was the *cause* of Hunter's many visits to the Evergreen High School ballfield?

4. What was the *cause* of Greg's feelings about his stepfather?

ANALYZING CHARACTERS

1. Which word could *not* be used to describe Vic Hunter? Explain your thinking.
   - *lawbreaker*
   - *vicious*
   - *deadbeat*

2. Which word could *not* be used to describe Mrs. Naylor? Support your opinion with an example.
   - *secretive*
   - *wealthy*
   - *protective*

3. Which word could *not* be used to describe Greg? Tell why you think so.
   - *hopeful*
   - *industrious*
   - *unforgiving*

VOCABULARY

1. Ric lost his job as a truck driver after he was charged with DUI. What does the acronym *DUI* mean?

2. Mr. Beverly fired Adam Lewis because he "wasn't cutting the mustard." What is meant by the idiom *to cut the mustard*?

3. Greg thought that Lewis would "relish" a chance to take revenge on him. What is the meaning of the verb *relish*?